By Richard Shelton

Books:

The Tattooed Desert
Of All the Dirty Words
Calendar
Among the Stones
You Can't Have Everything
The Bus to Veracruz
Selected Poems: 1969-1981
Hohokam

Chapbooks:

Journal of Return
The Heroes of Our Time
Chosen Place
Desert Water
A Kind of Glory

The
Other
Side of the
Story

The
Other
Side of the
Story

Richard Shelton

A James R. Hepworth Book

Confluence Press, Inc. / 1987

Copyright © 1987 by Richard Shelton

ISBN 0-917652-61-4 Cloth / 0-917652-62-2 Paper
Library of Congress Card Number 87-70926

Published by:

Confluence Press, Inc.
Lewis Clark State College
8th Avenue & 6th Street
Lewiston, Idaho 83501

Distributed to the trade by:

Kampmann & Company
9 East 40th Street
New York, New York 10016

Acknowledgements

Publication of this book is made possible by grants from the Idaho Commission on the Arts, a State agency, and the National Endowment for the Arts in Washington, D.C., a Federal agency.

"The Bus To Veracruz" and "The Monster" originally appeared in *The Antioch Review*; "The Messenger" and "The Swimmers" in *Chowder Review*; "Prophecy, Poetry, and the Camel's Nose" in *Field*; "Ghost Story" in *The Gramercy Review*; "The Wrong Room" in *Moon Pony*; and "The Hole" and "Here In Ecuador" in *The Ohio Review*.

"Prophecy, Poetry, and the Camel's Nose," "The Messenger," "The Stones," "The Monster," "Sleep," and "Doing Without" are reprinted from *You Can't Have Everything*, University of Pittsburgh Press. Copyright © 1975 by Richard Shelton.

"The Bus to Veracruz" and "The Swimmers" are reprinted from *The Bus To Veracruz*, University of Pittsburgh Press. Copyright © 1978 by Richard Shelton.

Typesetting and Design by Tanya Gonzales

Contents

Plot

Prophecy, Poetry, and the Camel's Nose

He called himself a prophet-poet and was employed in the household of a minor king who ruled one of the small eastern provinces at the edge of the desert. We no longer remember the prophet-poet's name, but we always tell his story to our children, as our fathers told it to us. And while the story is only a legend based on one very old and unreliable document, it is probably true. Certainly it is too bizarre to have been made up.

His duties as a prophet were to foretell the sex of each of the king's unborn children and the outcome of any battle in which the king might wish to engage. As a poet, he was expected to provide a poem for each wedding in the royal family and for other ceremonies and feast days. But his prophecies were always inaccurate, and his poetry was of such little merit that it loses nothing in translation.

In fact, his long poems were so painfully tedious

to listeners that the king finally established a decree making it unlawful to read poetry in public, a decree which was received by the people with such overwhelming approval that the prohibition spread to neighboring countries where it has remained in effect to this day. And although it is not for this reason we still remember the prophet-poet, other men have been honored by history for accomplishing less.

Eventually, because of an erroneous prophecy, the king became engaged in a disastrous war with a wild tribe of barbarians to the north. The king's forces were overcome, and the victorious barbarians, whose imaginations were developed only in the areas of violence and torture, entered the palace. Hearing the screams of the captives from his hiding place in the privy, the prophet-poet decided to relinquish his position as factotum to the king. He slipped behind the palisades and escaped on a one-eyed camel—straight into the desert.

It was rumored that beyond the desert lay the sea, and today we know this is true, but in those days no one knew what lay beyond the desert because no one had ever crossed it. And so, having abandoned himself to the desert, the prophet-poet had little hope of survival. Shortly after midday when his small supply of water was gone, he put a pebble in his mouth to allay his thirst. That night when the camel would go no farther, the exhausted traveller dismounted and fell on the ground, remembering only to spit out the pebble so he would not strangle on it in his sleep.

When he woke in the morning, he discovered the camel drinking at a small stream flowing from the sand near where the pebble had fallen. After quenching his thirst from the stream and eating some of the bread and cheese he carried with him, he felt much better and began to consider all the possible and impossible combinations of

chance or mischance by which this miracle had occurred. He could come to no conclusion except that the
pebble, with which he had been so intimately associated
on the previous day, was in some way responsible for the
presence of the stream, that it had somehow attracted
the water. Then with the boldness and logic character-
istic of saints and idiots, he popped the pebble back into
his mouth, filled his small water skin, mounted his
camel, and started off again further into the desert.

And it happened exactly as he had expected, as if he
were, after all, a true prophet. Each night he dropped the
pebble on the ground, and each morning when he woke
he found a small stream seeping from the desert floor
nearby. He was so pleased that every morning he rode on
with great cheer, reciting one or the other of his long poems, the sound of which was only slightly improved by
the fact that he carried the precious pebble always in his
mouth.

After many days he came to the sea and was rescued by
a ship which took him to a distant land. What became of
the one-eyed camel we do not know; but we know that
the prophet-poet lived in exile long enough to write a
thirty-two volume poem called "The Journey of the
Pebble," and that a copy of this poem eventually found
its way back to the desert he had crossed.

For within a few weeks of his journey, others also
ventured into the desert out of necessities no less
desperate than his had been, and soon a group of them
discovered the small stream at the spot where he had
spent the first night. Then the second stream was discovered, and the third. Within a few years it was known
that there were many streams in the desert, each spaced
one day's journey from the other, and that the traveller
who went from one to the next would be following an er-
ratic line, sometimes veering to the north and sometimes
to the south, but leading inevitably to the sea.

Fugitives who escaped from the war-torn eastern provinces settled near these streams and planted date groves and olive trees. The oases they created became small communities which supplied food and shelter to merchant caravans from many lands, for this was the only route to and from the coast. And gradually the small communities prospered and became cities. The streams were expanded and directed into systems of canals which furnished water for miles of farmland, vineyards, and groves. Nor have the people of these cities ever engaged in war, since it has always been obvious that each city is merely a link in a chain stretching across the desert from the inland provinces to the sea, and that if trade between any two of the cities should fail, the chain would be broken and they would all perish.

It is not beyond the bounds of modesty to say that we who live in the Cities of the Pebble are blessed above others. Not only have we been permitted to live in peace, but we have learned much from the travellers who follow the road past our doors. In order to trade, we have learned many languages, and our schools are often models for schools in other lands. Our craftsmen and artists are famous throughout the world. We have developed cotton of the finest quality known to man, and our fabric dyes, made from certain desert plants which grow nowhere else, are quite literally worth their weight in gold.

And we do not consider it a blot on our record that we have produced no great prophets or poets. Prophets sometimes visit our cities but never stay very long since no one pays the slightest attention to them. They soon decide that if they are going to be without honor anyway, they might as well go home. As for poets, our law which does not permit poetry to be read aloud in public is probably the reason why so few of our citizens attempt to follow that vocation. And those poets who pass through our cities, upon finding they will not be able to perform before audiences, usually leave quickly.

We accept the name "Cities of the Pebble" as the consequence of poetic error and because it has been handed down for many generations. But we, who have lived all our lives surrounded by the desert, know that a camel—even a one-eyed camel—can smell water many miles away. And we know that if given his head in the desert, a camel will lead the traveller to a place, and there are such places, where water lies very near the surface, although it cannot be detected by men. We also know that a camel will dig with his strong toes all night if necessary to reach the underground stream which his infallible nose has told him is there. So we believe in neither prophecy nor poetry, but place our trust in our own hard work and the noses of our camels.

The Messenger

There was no question of waiting for daylight, and I had expected the cold, but not the creaking as some unseen engine hoisted a damaged moon into the sky. Then I saw moulting angels, like scarecrows, standing in the fields while their feathers blew in drifts across the road. But none of this could stop me. I had memorized the message. I had sworn to deliver it. And it would prevent an execution scheduled for dawn.

When I arrived at the gates of the city, they were closed for the night. I beat on them with my fists. Pigeons rose with a clatter of wings and circled above, but nobody came to open the gates. So I searched for crevices between the stones and began to climb the wall. The fear of heights rode my back like a terrified child with its arms too tight on my throat, but at last I reached the top of the wall and descended into the city, my message secure and my fingers bleeding.

Then I ran down dark streets, slippery where night-jars had been emptied, and past barred windows behind which the rich and poor lay dreaming. I envied them their sleep. And as I passed one doorway, I smelled sickness and heard someone call out. It seemed like my name. But I ran on with each breath burning deeper in my chest. I told myself to keep going, keep going, you must do this one thing.

And I found the place, almost by instinct. It was in the center of the city, a large public building, ancient and formidable, with a courtyard where a crowd had gathered around a fire. I went straight to the fire, and the people made room for me. I could see their faces. From time to time they looked up at one lighted window above, and at those times their eyes were as dim as lanterns in distant trees.

But just as I was beginning to feel the warmth of the fire, a fat guard came up and demanded my papers. I told him I didn't have any. Then he asked for my name. In my fear and confusion I told him I didn't have a name either. He laughed, slapping his huge belly, and as he walked away, still laughing, the shield hanging on his back reflected light on the crowd around me. They were laughing too, and their faces were strange and contorted. But above their laughter I could hear another sound. It was as familiar as the squeal of a rusty hinge or the cry of an infant, but I could not identify it. It might have been a wolf howling on the slopes outside the city, or a woman in labor in one of the neighboring houses. I could not tell.

A man in the crowd stared at me with hard eyes and asked if I had come to give evidence at the trial. I told him I was a stranger in the city, that I had stopped to warm myself by the fire on a cold night, that I didn't know anything about it. Then a servant girl came to the lighted window and emptied a basin of water which ran over the stones of the courtyard, and everyone scrambled to avoid it. In the firelight it looked like blood. And I heard the sound again. Perhaps a whip descending or the cry of someone in pain.

Then a woman approached me, smiling. Her teeth were rotten; her breath stank of old wine. She made secret signs, offering me her body, and she led me to an aisle where the horses were tethered. When she undressed, her body was ugly; but I lay with her to prove I could observe the customs of the city. And as we got up from the dirty straw, I heard the sound again. This time I was sure it was a human voice, and I asked the woman if she knew who had cried out. But she looked at me strangely and said it was only the cock crowing to warn us of approaching dawn. Then we returned to the fire, and I saw shadows moving behind the lighted window as if a procession were passing from the room, down a stairway lit by torches, and out into the earliest light of morning. But I remained in the courtyard with the other messengers.

We warm our hands at the fire and salvage what comfort we can from dawn and the news of distant disasters. We have heard rumors of cataclysms, of storms, and of the darkening sun in other places. But we have been here for years, and the road no longer remembers the sound of our feet. Each morning we return from sleep as if from a long journey, forgetting the messages we have memorized and sworn to deliver in our dreams. Forgetting even our dreams, the unspeakable solutions to problems we no longer have.

The Bus
to Veracruz

The mail is slow here. If I died, I wouldn't find out about
it for a long time. Perhaps I am dead already. At any rate,
I am living in the wrong tense of a foreign language and
have almost no verbs and only a few nouns to prove I exist. When I need a word, I fumble among the nouns and
find one, but so many are similar in size and color. I am
apt to come up with *caballo* instead of *caballero*, or *carne*
instead of *casa*. When that happens, I become confused
and drop the words. They roll across the tile floor in all
directions. Then I get down on my hands and knees and
crawl through a forest of legs, reaching under tables and
chairs to retrieve them. But I am no longer embarrassed
about crawling around on the floor in public places. I
have come to realize that I am invisible most of the time
and have been since I crossed the border.

All the floors are tile. All the tiles are mottled with the

same disquieting pattern in one of three muddy colors—shades of yellow, purple, or green. They make me think of dried vomit, desiccated liver, and scum on a pond. The floor of my room is dried vomit with a border of scum on a pond, and like most of the floors it has several tiles missing, which is a great blessing to me. These lacunae are oases in the desert where I can rest my eyes. The nausea from which I suffer so much of the time is not caused by the food or water, but by the floors. I know this because when I sit in the town square, which is covered with concrete of no particular color, the nausea subsides.

The town is small, although larger than it would seem to a visitor—if there were any visitors—and remote. It has no landing field for even small planes, and the nearest railroad is almost one hundred kilometers to the east. The only bus goes to Veracruz. Often I stop at the bus terminal to ask about the bus to Veracruz. The floor of the bus terminal is scum on a pond with a border of desiccated liver, but there are many tiles missing. The terminal is always deserted except for Rafael and Esteban, sometimes sitting on the bench inside, some-times lounging just outside the door. They are young, barefoot, and incredibly handsome. I buy them Cocas from the machine, and we have learned to communicate in our fashion. When I am with them, I am glad to be in-visible, glad that they never look directly at me. I could not bear the soft vulnerability of those magnificent eyes.

"When does the bus leave for Veracruz?" I ask them. I have practiced this many times and am sure I have the right tense. But the words rise to the ceiling, burst, and fall as confetti around us. A few pieces catch in their dark hair and reflect the light like jewels. Rafael rubs his foot on the floor. Esteban stares out the filthy window. Are they sad, I wonder, because they believe there is no bus to Veracruz or because they don't know when it leaves.

14

"Is there a bus to Veracruz?" Suddenly they are happy again. Their hands fly like vivacious birds. *"Si, hay! Por supuesto, Senor! Es verdad!"* They believe, truly, in the bus to Veracruz. Again I ask them when it leaves. Silence and sadness. Rafael studies one of the tiles on the floor as if it contains the answer. Esteban turns back to the window. I buy them *Cocas* from the machine and go away.

Once a week I stop at the post office to get my mail from the ancient woman in the metal cage, and each week I receive one letter. Actually, the letters are not mine, and the ancient woman has probably known this for a long time, but we never speak of it and she continues to hand me the letters, smiling and nodding in her coquettish way, eager to please me. Her hair is braided with colored ribbons, and her large silver earrings jingle when she bobs her head, which she does with great enthusiasm when I appear. I could not estimate how old she is. Perhaps even she has forgotten. But she must have been a great beauty at one time. Now she sits all day in the metal cage in the post office, a friendly apparition whose bright red lipstick is all the more startling because she has no teeth.

The first time I entered the post office, it was merely on an impulse to please her. I was expecting no mail, since no one knew where I was. But each time I passed, I had seen her through the window, seated in her metal cage with no customers to break the monotony. She always smiled and nodded at me through the window, eager for any diversion. Finally one day I went in on the pretext of calling for my mail, although I knew there would be none. To avoid the confusion which my accent always causes, I wrote my name on a slip of paper and presented it to her. Her tiny hands darted among the pigeonholes, and to my astonishment she presented me with a letter which was addressed to me in care of general delivery.

She was so delighted with her success that I simply took the letter and went away, unwilling to disillusion her.

As soon as I opened the letter, the mystery was solved. My name is fairly common. The letter was intended for someone else with the same name. It was written on blue paper, in flawless Palmer Method script, and signed by a woman. It was undated and there was no return address. But it was in English, and I read it shamelessly, savoring each phrase. I rationalized by convincing myself that the mail was so slow the man to whom the letter had been written was probably already dead and could not object to my reading his mail. But I knew before I finished the letter that I would return to the post office later on the chance there might be others. She loved him. She thought he was still alive.

Since then I have received one letter each week, to the enormous delight of my ancient friend in the post office. I take the letters home and steam them open, careful to leave no marks on the delicate paper. They are always from the same woman, and I feel by now that I know her. Sometimes I dream about her, as if she were someone I knew in the past. She is blond and slender, no longer young but far from old. I can see her long, graceful fingers holding the pen as she writes, and sometimes she reaches up to brush a strand of hair away from her face. Even that slight gesture has the eloquence of a blessing.

When I have read each letter until I can remember it word for word, I reseal it. Then, after dark, I take it back to the post office by a circuitous route, avoiding anyone who might be on the street at that hour. The post office is always open, but the metal cage is closed and the ancient one is gone for the night. I drop the letter into the dead letter box and hurry away.

At first I had no curiosity about what happened to the letters after they left my hands. Then I began to wonder if they were destroyed or sent to some central office where, in an attempt to locate the sender and return them, someone might discover that they had been opened. Still later, the idea that some nameless official in a distant city might be reading them became almost unbearable to me. It was more and more difficult to remember that they were not my letters. I could not bear to think of anyone else reading her words, sensing her hesitations and tenderness. At last I decided to find out.

It took months of work, but with practice I became clever at concealing myself in shadowy doorways and watching. I have learned that once each week a nondescript man carrying a canvas bag enters the post office through the back door, just as the ancient woman is closing her metal cage for the night. She empties the contents of the dead letter box into his canvas bag, and he leaves by the door he came in. The man then begins a devious journey which continues long into the night. Many nights I have lost him and have had to begin again the following week. He doubles back through alleys and down obscure streets. Several times he enters deserted buildings by one door and emerges from another. He crosses the cemetery and goes through the Cathedral.

But finally he arrives at his destination—the bus terminal. And there, concealed behind huge doors which can be raised to the ceiling, is the bus to Veracruz. The man places his canvas bag in the luggage compartment, slams the metal cover with a great echoing clang, and goes away.

And later, at some unspecified hour, the bus to Vera-cruz rolls silently out of the terminal, a luxury liner leaving port with all its windows blazing. It has three yellow lights above the windshield and three gold stars along each side. The seats are red velvet and there are gold tassels between the windows. The dashboard is draped with brocade in the richest shades of yellow, purple, and green; and on this alter is a statue of the Virgin, blond and shimmering. Her slender fingers are extended to bless all those who ride the bus to Veracruz, but the only passenger is an ancient woman with silver earrings who sits by the window, nodding and smiling to the empty seats around her. There are two drivers who take turns during the long journey. They are young and incredibly handsome, with eyes as soft as the wings of certain luminous brown moths.

The bus moves through sleeping streets without making a sound. When it gets to the highway, it turns toward Veracruz and gathers speed. Then nothing can stop it: not the rain, nor the washed-out bridges, nor the sharp mountain curves, nor the people who stand by the road to flag it down.

I believe in the bus to Veracruz. And someday, when I am too tired to struggle any longer with the verbs and nouns, when the ugliness and tedium of this place overcome me, I will be on it. I will board the bus with my ticket in my hand. The doors of the terminal will rise to the ceiling, and we will move out through the darkness, gathering speed, like a great island of light.

Setting

The Hole

I have dug a hole. It is not an extremely large hole, about four feet across and perhaps three feet deep; but it is a wonderful hole, a magnificent hole. I was planning to encase it in concrete and fill it with water to make a pool, a trap for goldfish. But once I had seen the hole, once I became aware of the *holeness* of it, I could not bear to destroy it. It exists and has a function: to be a hole. It has as much right to exist as a mountain or a tree. And I have gotten over the notion that I created it. It was there from the beginning, waiting to be uncovered. I merely found it.

Everything conspires to destroy a hole. Leaves blow into it. Sand and water creep in to fill it. And people have an overpowering urge to throw things into it: stones, trash, cigarette butts, anything. When they have nothing to throw into it, they often fall into it. They seem unable to leave it alone, as if it were something evil, something threatening. But a hole is the least aggressive of things. It asks only to exist and to be what it is.

So I am building a wall around the hole to help protect it. Tourists will go to see anything; and when they come to see my hole, I will put up a sign which says: NO PART OF THIS HOLE MAY BE REMOVED UPON PENALTY OF LAW. There is no law to protect holes; but it will be a small deception which harms no one, and holes need all the help they can get.

A hole is only distantly related to a cave, although it might appear that a cave is just a hole lying down. Actually, in the hierarchy of negative space, holes have much more status than caves. Holes are more courageous, exposing themselves to constant danger, while caves hide under their roofs and protective banks. And people do not seem to have the urge to destroy caves. We simply explore them and deface them. But when we encounter a hole, we want to fill it.

And while each hole is a quite distinct hole, all have two things in common. They love shadows and sound. They hold shadows as long as they can,caressing them. And they do the same thing with sounds, especially the sound of a voice. When I speak into the hole, it cherishes and amplifies my voice, reluctant to let it go. The hole seems quite grateful when it has the opportunity to roll words around, enhancing them in subtle ways. And it takes no real effort for me to throw it a few words now and then. I rather enjoy talking to it. I have come to admire the way it takes pride in being what it is—not the absence of anything, but the presence of something—a hole.

But where is the surface of a hole? I once believed that the surface of a hole is level with the surface of the ground around it. From observation I have come to realize that this is not true. The earth has a surface, and the sea has a surface, but a hole has no surface. A hole has only sides and a bottom from which it extends infinitely upward, like a shaft of light; and as the earth revolves, it moves with great care and precision between the stars.

The Stones

I love to go out on summer nights and watch the stones grow. I think they grow better here in the desert, where it is warm and dry, than almost anywhere. Or perhaps it is only that the young ones are more active here.

Young stones tend to move about more than their elders consider good for them. Most young stones have a secret desire which their parents had before them but have forgotton ages ago. And because this desire involves water, it is never mentioned. The older stones disapprove of water and say, "Water is a gadfly who never stays in one place long enough to learn anything." But the young stones try to work themselves into a position, slowly and without their elders noticing it, in which a sizable stream of water during a summer storm might catch them broadside and unknowing, so to speak, and push them along over a slope or down an arroyo. In spite of the danger this involves, they want to travel and see something of the world and settle in a new place, far from home, where they can raise their own dynasties away from the domination of their parents.

And although family ties are very strong among stones, many of the more daring young ones have succeeded; and they carry scars to prove to their children that they once went on a journey, helter—skelter and high water, and traveled perhaps fifteen feet, an incredible distance. As they grow older, they cease to brag about such clandestine adventures.

It is true that old stones get to be very conservative. They consider all movement either dangerous or downright sinful. They remain comfortably where they are and often get fat. Fatness, as a matter of fact, is a mark of distinction.

And on summer nights, after the young stones are asleep, the elders turn to a serious and frightening subject—the moon, which is always spoken of in whispers. "See how it glows and whips across the sky, always changing its shape," one says. And another says, "Feel how it pulls at us, urging us to follow." And a third whispers, "It is a stone gone mad."

South Paradise

'Ride, boldly, ride,'
The shade replied,
'If you seek for Eldorado.'

—Edgar Allen Poe

Paradise is more beautiful than anything we could have imagined, but the brochures lied. It wasn't the heat so much as the humidity, and the air...well, there wasn't any. It had rained, was raining, and was about to rain. The natives blame the government for this. They blame the government for everything. The truth is, there is no government. It is only a convenience the natives invented long ago to explain the way things were, since religious beliefs no longer served that function. They also believe that the government is planning to trade the entire country to the United States in return for the cancellation of a huge national debt which has been growing each year. They have no idea what happened to the money, but are philosophical about being traded to another country, believing that one government is as good as another. The important thing is to have one in order to have something to blame.

As I said, most of the country is incredibly beautiful,

25

but the coast is a disappointment. Someone, undoubtedly the government, had poured too much oil on troubled waters and the sea had congealed. An island floated just offshore like a pyramid on a lake of grease. One frigate bird revolved above it with still wings, a black dagger suspended by an invisible thread. Generations of dead fish rotted on the beach. We felt exposed, not to anything in particular, but exposed as the negative of a photograph is exposed.

The natives are exceedingly handsome and languid, all gesture without motion. They pose in the shade on the porches of their *jalapas*, too picturesque to move. Cannas the color of blood bloom at their feet, and above them the flame trees flame. They wear white and slumber like indolent angels while the world burns. They did not look at us but at something behind us, something amusing and strange, perhaps a shadow with nothing to cause it. Their dogs came out to greet us, small and covered with sores, wagging their entire emaciated bodies.

My knowledge of the language is slight, but I made them understand that we were trying to find the Hotel Eldorado, the one with *aire acondicionado.* "It is on the road which circles the bay," several of them told us. I explained, as best I could, that the road which circled the bay was flooded and impassable. "Then the hotel is on the highway to the Capital," they all replied. "Seven kilometers along the highway to the Capital is located the tourist hotel, *muy grande, muy rico.*" "But does it have *aire acondicionado?*" They were all offended. "*Como si!*" Of course it has *aire acondicionado!* They withdrew their attention from us in order to resume their contemplation of something profound, probably the government, and we who worship machines went off through the rain in search of Eldorado.

Seven kilometers down the road to the Capital, in a swamp, we found the ruins of a large, unfinished structure abandoned for years. It was inhabited by snakes and tarantulas and covered with purple bougainvillea so lush it made us nauseous. We suffered from beauty and dysentery, and could find no relief from either. There was no Hotel Eldorado. There was no *aire acondicionado.* There were disciplined armies of mosquitoes, ravenous enough to have eaten even the natives' dogs if we had brought them with us, and they had wanted to come.

So we went on through a perfect landscape: somnolent white villages of thatched huts hidden in the flowers, hibiscus with yellow blossoms the size of dinner plates, orchids hanging from the trees, with here and there a huge pink sow lying beside the road, gleaming like porcelain. It was magnificent, but we fled on and on, exhausted, in search of some place with *aire acondicionado,* in search of any place but the paradise we were in, utterly beautiful, designed by some god who had never been there and did not plan to go.

Ghost Story

A woman in a white dress stands near the road. It is evening under the dark trees. She has come from her house in the distance to mail a letter. Her hair is blowing in the wind. As we drive past, she waves shyly with the letter in her hand. She puts the letter in the mailbox and raises the flag.

Our eyes return to the road, but we cannot remember our destination or where we have been. Slowly a silver moon rises, a coin with a face we recognize as we recognized the face of the woman near the road, as we knew what the letter contained. It is a letter to her lover who has gone away, we do not know where. It says all her hopes are for his return. It says she is lonely and sometimes waves to strangers driving past.

We follow the road, remembering a face beside a mailbox, a letter, a pale hand, a smile more beautiful than we have ever known. The hand waves. The house is unseen beyond dark trees in a place to which no one ever returns. We think we must go back and speak to her, but we are strangers, and by now she has walked up the lane toward the house. The wind blows on and on.

The Wrong Room

When I opened the door, I saw a window in the far wall directly in front of me; and through it I could see a full moon rising. The walls of the room were white, and there was a bright patch of moonlight on the floor. Everything was exactly where it should have been, where I remembered it—the bed in the corner and beside it an oval rug. Against the wall to the right a chair and a tall chest. To the left a small table with a long cloth and a covered birdcage hanging above it.

Then, as I waited for my eyes to adjust to the partial darkness, it seemed the objects in the room were moving slowly toward me, as if the floor were tilting. The bed and rug were moving away from the far wall, and the chest and chair were now closer to the door through which I had just entered. The patch of moonlight, also, was creeping across the floor.

At once I realized that this illusion was caused by the shadows of things, which were lengthening as the moon rose. I went to the window to look out, but discovered that the window was painted on the wall. There was no window. And the moon was a round mirror in the center of the painted window, reflecting light from the hallway where I had left the door open.

As I turned back in confusion, I noticed the zebra in front of the closet. He had just removed his stripes and was standing in the moonlight in his underwear. I was in the wrong room. We were both embarrassed. I apologized for the intrusion and left as quickly as possible, closing the door behind me.

Here In Ecuador

for Tom Miller

I want to know if Tom Tom was really the piper's son. Was he legitimate or a bastard? And why did he steal the pig? Was he hungry or was he attracted to pigs? Did anybody ask the pig about it? Surely pigs have some rights, even in foreign countries.

Here in Ecuador, pigs go anywhere they want to and are an integral part of society. Such a theft would not have been allowed to go unpunished. The pigs in Ecuador squeal when they are being stolen. They squeal like nothing else you have ever heard, and somebody comes running, usually a policeman with a nasty-looking gun. My advice is to stay away from pigs in Ecuador. No matter how much they attract you, keep your hands off them. And if you are in Ecuador and your name happens to be Tom Tom, change it to something less controversial like César or Alejandro. That's my advice.

I would also like to know what happened to the pig after Tom Tom ran away. It must have been a very small pig, probably a piglet, or the little bastard couldn't have carried it. In Ecuador the pigs get very big. Some of them get so big it takes five men to persuade one of them to get out of the middle of the road when traffic is heavy. Usually they prefer to lie in the middle of the road where the mud is deepest, and they care nothing about traffic. There isn't much traffic anyway except during a war, and pigs do not acknowledge wars. Wars are not on their agendas. If pigs happen to be going somewhere, they walk through wars; otherwise they sleep through them or wallow through them. Actually, pigs are natural noncombatants, and everyone in Ecuador recognizes this. Not only are pigs smart enough to adopt this political attitude, they are clever enough to get away with it. For this reason they are universally respected here in Ecuador, where we have had many wars and have lost all of them.

Most of our houses are built on stilts, and the pigs live under the houses where it is cool and moist. If a house is not on stilts, the pigs live inside the house, which is only proper since the owner did not have the forethought to build the house on stilts for the pigs' comfort. If you happen to be sleeping on the floor of a house not built on stilts, the pigs make good company at night. Their snoring is rythmic and musical and helps you sleep peacefully. But when they appear to be sleeping, pigs are actually thinking deep thoughts which bring pleasant dreams to the entire household.

They think about eternity, and realize it is now and everywhere. They think about the future and the past, and they realize it is all one thing and it is within them. They know they are immortal. They are in no hurry. If you look deep into a pig's little eye, you will see something of what they know. It is everything and nothing and goes on forever. It transcends all human knowledge.

Pigs love to rub against things, and they love to have things rubbed against them. It reminds them of the here and now, which is part of eternity. Each time we rub a pig with a stick, we become part of its eternity, and the pig loves us. The pig dozes off into eternity, and we go along for the ride. This might last only a few seconds or forever. It does not matter. The small eyes close, the great heart beats more slowly, the stick moves back and forth, the world ends, the world begins again as it has always done. Something crawls out of the sea, something crawls into the mud, something scratches against a stick, the sky opens, the mud deepens, the pig is willing. In Ecuador these things are understood. If you want to see eternity, look in a pig's eye.

Character

The Monster

I have a singular talent: the ability to make old women cry. Whenever I see one, I say to her, "Something is lost and since I have never seen it, I despair of finding it. Please help me! There is no one else for me to turn to."

She begins to search frantically, not knowing for what, and she finds various things. A darning egg, a bus token, a stiffened shoe, a ceramic bird. And she holds these things up to me one by one, saying, "Is this it? Is this?" And each time I shake my head sadly. Sooner or later she comes upon the one thing she has hidden from herself, the thing she has successfully forgotten. A tiny spoon, a necklace with a broken clasp, a sea shell. And when she finds it, she begins to cry.

Sleep

We are time and it is not the
years that pass but we ourselves.

—Octavio Paz

There is an old man I dream about every night. He is ugly and his breath stinks. He walks up to me and says, "Drop dead!" I say, "Bug off, old man!" He says, "Drop dead!" I say...well, you get the picture. This goes on all night. I wake up every morning exhausted. I guess he sleeps during the day, getting ready for the nightly battle. He never seems to tire of it. I try staying awake to avoid him, but as soon as I slip over the edge, he appears. "Drop dead!" "Bug off, old man!" And on it goes.

Lately I have come to believe he is somebody I know or remember from the past. I look for him all the time. I go to bingo games and stare at each face. I hang around rest homes. Sometimes I wear a white coat and pretend I work there; sometimes I just sneak in and watch television in the lobby among drooping chins and complaining intestines. But I never find him. He is too clever for me. I walk through parks in the afternoon and have begun to frequent certain bars where the dead mingle with the dying and nobody makes distinctions.

And each night he returns. "Drop dead!" he says. "Bug off, old man!" I tell him. It's a helluva way to live. I drink more now than I should, and sometimes it almost works. When he comes he is vague and staggering, and his speech is not clear, but he comes anyway. And sometimes I almost think I recognize that drunken face: eyes like a battlefield after a war, and the ruins of what must have been an irresistible smile.

It isn't all bad. I've gotten to know some of the old ones. I kind of enjoy the bingo; it's fun if you win. And they seem to like me. Sometimes during commercials we talk about things. Nothing much, but things. They listen when I tell them about my problem and how tired I am because I don't sleep well. They seem to understand, and nobody else did. I even forget to look for him among them, since it's been so long and I haven't found him.

As a matter of fact, I've kind of settled in with them, I guess. I know it's strange for anyone my age to spend his afternoons in the park and his evening watching television in an old folk's home. I could be out dancing tonight if I wanted to, but this is more comfortable, and I have friends here. I couldn't just desert them, could I?

And it's odd, these last few years he doesn't come anymore in my dreams. Lately it's been a young man who bobs in, bright and shiny and kind of friendly, with an irresistible smile, like somebody I knew but can't remember. And he says, "Don't forget me." And I say, "Let me sleep, young man!" And he says, "Sleep, old friend, you have won the battle." And I sleep.

Brief Communications
from My Widowed Mother

You remember I told you I hired an old geazer from church to paint the outside of the house. Well, I'm sure glad he's finally finished. What a pain in the neck. I made the mistake of inviting him in for coffee once in awhile and he would just set around and grin like a skunk eating horse manure. The last day he was here he said I was a mighty fine-looking lady and he thought the two of us should get "hitched," that's what he said, "hitched," and share our "declining years." You could have knocked me over with a feather. Declining years my Aunt Hattie! All he wanted was to get his hands on my pension checks. But I fixed him. I just laughed like it was a big joke and told him to come back when he had a million dollars and a VERY SERIOUS heart condition. That's the only kind of man I'm interested in declining with. And he isn't a very good painter anyway.

—

I read that book you gave me. It was terrible—the dirtiest book I ever read. It's disgusting what they can get printed these days. Have you got any more by the same author?

—

Your sister has been lying about her age so long even her husband doesn't know how old she is. He must think she was about ten when he married her. I told her if she doesn't quit lying about her age she'll never get any social security.

—

You remember Harry, the old drunk who lives up the street. Yesterday he was staggering home from the bus stop drunk as a lord. He got right in front of my house and fell down and started vomiting all over himself. Then he passed out and all the stray dogs in the neighborhood ran out and started licking his face. It was positively revolting. I had to call the police AND the dogcatcher.

—

I'm still having those fainting spells but the doctor can't do anything about them. Two weeks ago I fainted in church. Deacon Carson had to carry me out right in front of everybody. It was terrible. My hat fell off and my hair must have looked a fright. It caused quite a commotion and I got a nice write-up in the church bulletin. Said I was feeling better now. Ha!

—

Your cousin is always just about to get a job, but he never gets one. I think he's too preoccupied to work.

—

Those two young boys who moved in next door are driving me crazy. Loud music all the time and I can smell the marajawana smoke clear over here. Lots of friends

44

coming and going all the time, mostly girls. Last week they had an orgie. I'm not kidding. I was out in the back yard and I looked through the hedge and there was this young couple naked and DOING IT right out on the lawn. It was disgusting. After they finished I came in and called the police. You'd better believe I'm going to keep my eyes open from now on. They're not going to get away with that sort of thing around here.

—

One of the neighbors up the street went completely besmirch last Saturday night and killed his wife. It's getting so only the widows are safe in this neighborhood.

—

Last week a lady's car broke down in front of the house. A big sort-of-round thing fell off the rear end. I went out to see if I could help her, but her car wouldn't start. I told her I thought it was her muffler although I don't know exactly what a muffler is used for but I remember years ago when the muffler fell off your father's old car and it looked something like that. So I invited her in to use the phone. She called the garage and told them her muffler fell off. They told her just to drive the car to the garage, but she told them it wouldn't start. So they said they would send a tow truck. We had a cup of coffee and a nice chat while she waited. Turned out she was a widow lady too. I told her she was mighty lucky to know how to drive so she didn't have to be dependent on everybody like I am. Pretty soon the tow truck came and the man got out and started laughing. He said, "Muffler, hell, Lady! Your gas tank fell off." You could have knocked me over with a feather.

—

My poor little dog is very sick and she's only seven years old. I took her to two vets and they don't know

45

what's wrong with her. They think it's something in her mind. I don't know what I would do without her. If she dies I guess I'll have to come visit you.

Love,

Mother

Doing Without

If I can bear your laughter, as you and your friends pass by in search of further pleasures, forgive me my silence. It indicates neither envy nor contempt, nor am I a Puritan. I am a Stoic in a land of Epicureans. I know your life is not all pleasure, just as I know there are two choices and both are valid. We can enjoy the strokes and take the licks that go with them, or we can do without. Any other path will lead to misery.

A good case can be made for doing without. Think of it not as a lack of companionship and pleasure, but as a lack of complicity and disappointment. And there will be animals. When they act as if they love you, for that moment at least, they love you. Nor will you find yourself by travelling from place to place. Instead, you will find other travellers, all avoiding themselves. Why not stay in one place and wait? It may take years, but so does travel.

47

First you must escape. When you hear someone calling your name, and there will be someone calling your name, look carefully in the wrong direction and walk on. Move into a small house on the outskirts of a town like Ely, Nevada. Live alone. Be courteous but distant to everyone you meet. Each of them will make up a story to explain your presence, and all will believe their own stories. You will be accepted. Those who do without are always accepted, since they do not ask to be loved.

Summer will follow spring. There will be difficult times in the winter. But years later, while thin bodies of smoke rise above the houses on the mountain, and snow is forgiving the ugly for its ugliness, the beautiful for its beauty, there will be long mornings of rapture when you can't remember your name. Such happiness can be endured if it is earned, and it is earned by doing without.

The Swimmers

If we go back to the old places, we will be happy again. Let us run away to Mexico and live in the upstairs room of the house by the sea. It will be a second honeymoon. Do you remember the old house by the sea? The beach and the two young swimmers?

They have given us up, the young swimmers. They have left us behind. We did not love them enough; we did not cherish them enough. But sometimes at night they come to us through the snow, down the dirty sidestreet, pale and shivering, a little drunk, carrying flowers. And we hear their laughter in the next room, like bells under water. We think they are happy, but later we hear them crying softly in the hall.

Let us go back to the house by the sea. From its tall windows we will look west across the Pacific. We will watch the young swimmers going out farther each day.

One day they will not return. That night we will celebrate on the beach with fireworks, aiming our Roman candles at a point just above the horizon. One of our rockets will bloom like a giant hibiscus and fall slowly, petal by petal, into the open hands of the dead.

Action

The Jericho Road

*A certain man went down from Jerusalem to Jericho,
and fell among thieves, which stripped him of his raiment,
and wounded him, and departed, leaving him half dead.
And by chance there came down a certain priest that way:
and when he saw him, he passed by on the other side. And
likewise a Levite, when he was at the place, came and
looked at him, and passed by on the other side. But a
certain Samaritan, as he journeyed, came where he was:
and when he saw him, he had compassion on him, and
went to him, and bound up his wounds, pouring in oil and
wine, and set him on his own beast, and brought him to an
inn, and took care of him. And on the morrow when he
departed, he took out two pence, and gave them to the
host, and said unto him, take care of him; and whatsoever
thou spendest more, when I come again, I will repay thee.*

During the reign of Herod Agrippa I, who was a lover of
pleasure and sport and had devoted most of his time to
building amphitheaters in Caesarea and in the other new
Hellenistic cities on the Mediterranean Coast, the old
road between Jerusalem and Jericho, far inland, became
so notorious for banditry that no one would venture upon

it without an armed escort of many men. And even when accompanied by such an escort, some travellers did not reach their destinations, since the men they hired to protect them might well be bandits in disguise.

There were also the dreaded Sicarii, the Long Knives, who could appear out of the desert more quickly than a sandstorm and who were thought to have political motives, although they were not always selective in terms of their victims. After stripping a group of travellers of all valuables, the Sicarii were noted for multilating them with great dexterity and redistributing bodily parts with a kind of grisly humor, so that it was often difficult for those who found the victims to get their bodies properly assembled again.

Under these conditions, commerce between Jerusalem and Jericho languished, and although the two cities were only 120 furlongs apart, it became almost impossible to send even a message from one to the other. And so it was one of the first official acts of the New Administration of Procurators to send a Roman Centurion and his hundred soldiers to scourge the road of bandits. The Centurion's force was so diligent that within a few months there was no more banditry reported in the entire area, but still the people would not travel on the road because of its frightening reputation.

At this point the new Procurator whose stewardship centered on Jerusalem and the new Procurator whose stewardship centered on Jericho made a strong attempt to revive trade and tourism along a once-busy but by then deserted thoroughfare. They called in the services of the Royal Commission on Commerce. In a joint appeal to that body, they requested help in finding some way to overcome the fears of the people, not only the people in the two cities most concerned, but of people throughout the world, since news of the banditry had reached the ears of merchants as far away as Damascus and even Rome; and the merchants had rerouted their caravans accordingly. The Royal Commission on Commerce was made up of some of the most distinguished merchants, lawyers, military men, and government officials in the previous kingdom. It had been appointed many years earlier by the Emperor in order to stimulate commerce, taxable revenue, in a rather backward and unprofitable Tetrarchy. But under the reign of the late Agrippa I, who was more interested in banquets and colosseums than in commerce, it had never been encouraged to function. Now, suddenly brought out of obscurity, that ancient body assembled. Vacancies caused by death or senility were filled with new appointees; and all twenty members met in the refurbished chambers provided for them in one of the palaces Agrippa had built in Caesarea, where they had luxury, the sea breeze, and a magnificent view of the Mediterranean to help them deliberate.

Both Procurators appeared before them, and the Commission listened to the advice of dozens of experts. They consulted a famous soothsayer and two oracles, primarily to satisfy the Hellenistic leanings of some of their members, but from these could obtain no agreement. Finally, after six months of hard work, they drafted a document which outlined a three-phase plan. A copy of this document was presented to each of the Procurators, and it was read aloud before them at a closed session.

First, they proposed an educational campaign which would give the road a new image. Second, they advised that the road itself be vastly improved in order to make it more attractive to travellers. And third, they outlined a holiday spectacle on a brilliant scale, a Grand Opening of the new road to be staged with such showmanship it would convince the people that the road from Jerusalem to Jericho was not only safe, but that it was an altogether delightful thoroughfare. And in spite of the fact that the expense invloved in this plan would be considerable, the Procurators of Jerusalem and Jericho accepted it, relieved that something was finally going to be done about the road, which had been a source of great embarrassment to them.

In order to accomplish the first phase of the plan, the Royal Commission issued an official proclamation, copies of which were posted on the walls of many building in both cities and read aloud each day in the market places. The proclamation stated that the road from Jerusalem to Jericho had always been safe for travellers, and that its misleading reputation as a highway along which bandits lurked behind every bush and sand dune was the result of a long-standing plot to overthrow the government.

According to the proclamation, the original source of the road's false reputation was a story, which became widespread, concerning a traveller on the road to Jericho who was set upon by thieves, left for dead, and later befriended by a Samaritan. That story had been traced back to an itinerate false prophet of little reputation who had been discredited and ultimately executed near Jerusalem for his crimes, which included lying to public officials, blaspheming, destroying public trust, and undermining government policy. The proclamation further stated that since this false prophet's execution, evidence had come to light which indicated that he had been sent by an unfriendly foreign power to disrupt and paralyze commerce, thus making the country vulnerable to attack.

As soon as this educational campaign was underway, members of the Royal Commission turned their attention to the second phase of the plan, the improvement of the road itself. First, they realized, the name of the road would have to be changed. As *The Jericho Road* it had a fearful reputation, and as *The Jericho Road* it figured in the false prophet's story. A new name would remove it from such unfortunate associations.

Each of the Procurators secretly hoped that the road would be given his own name, and both attempted to bribe individual members of the Commission to that effect. But when it became obvious to the Commission that either Procurator would be mortally offended if the road were named in honor of the other, a lengthy debate ensued. Some members of the Commission suggested that the road from Jerusalem to a point halfway between the two cities should be named after the Procurator of Jerusalem, and from that point on to Jericho it should carry the name of the Procurator of Jericho. Others maintained that the west side of the road should be named after one Procurator and the east side after the other. There was also a strongly favored proposal to build a second road roughly parallel to the existing one so that each Procurator would have his own road.

Finally, after weeks of debate, the Commission decided to avoid these alternatives and to accept the name *The Royal Road*, although no one of royal blood had passed over the road for many years because members of the royal families in the area were not noted for bravery. But as the merchant who suggested this name pointed out to his fellow Commission members, it would make the people who travelled on the road feel important, and thus encourage tourism.

Even before the question of the name was settled, work had begun on the road. The plan called for it to be widened and resurfaced and for campsites, each large enough to accomodate several caravans, to be built and landscaped at intervals of twenty-four furlongs. Since much of the road led through desert country, flumes had to be constructed which would bring water from the Jordan and from the mountain springs northeast of the

57

road. As soon as the flumes were finished and water was diverted into them, whole crews of gardeners went to work at each campsite, turning these patches of desert into gardens, groves, and meadows.

The enormous expense of this construction and landscaping was shared by the two Procurators, who had levied special taxes to obtain funds. And the Commission was careful to see that the Procurators received major credit for the impressive project, word of which was beginning to spread throughout the country and even abroad. Nor were the members of the Commission idle while this work was underway. Each of them had further ideas for the improvement of *The Royal Road*. The first suggestion which went beyond their original plan was that a magnificent gate be built at either end of the road. Then one of the members thought it very important that each campsite have a large pool of constantly renewed water for bathing. Another felt that a complex of buildings should be erected at each campsite to house the vendors of food and supplies which the heavy traffic would undoubtedly attract. It would be a shame, he felt, to allow the vendors to sprawl in an unsightly array of tents and shacks, as they did elsewhere.

To this suggestion was added the idea that all the buildings along the road should be examples of the finest architecture the country could provide; and that no matter how utilitarian, they should have the grace and beauty of temples and should be decorated by the finest artists so that travellers on road would be constantly reminded of the Empire's artistic and cultural heritage. For, as one member of the Royal Commission pointed out, the Commission was not a narrowly materialistic body concerned only with commerce, but a group of men chosen because they understood that aesthetic and cultural activities were also essential to the health of the people and were, in fact, the foundation upon which commerce was built.

At first the two Procurators resisted these suggestions because of the added expense; but after several sessions with the Commission, they were convinced that the project should be extended beyond its original scope so that, without losing any of its practical and commercial advantages, it would produce a monument of which the Emperor could be proud. And they were convinced that *The Royal Road*, although it would take years to complete, would unite the people in national pride and attract thousands of traders and tourists from the entire world, all of whom would add to the revenues of the two cities. They also recognized the truth in what the Commission told them: that they would be spoken of by scholars and written about in the scrolls of history as the two far-sighted Procurators who had created *The Royal Road*, one of the wonders of the world. And certainly, as the Commission pointed out, it would do no harm to levy more taxes on a temporary basis, since the road would pay for itself during the first year of its use.

When the two Procurators were convinced of all this, even they began to add suggestions of their own. One wanted an elaborate fountain built at each of the campsites. The other thought that each fountain should include a statue depicting some memorable event in the history of Jerusalem or Jericho. And more suggestions from the Commission poured in.

One of these, readily accepted, called for a huge pavilion on each side of the road at a point exactly halfway between the two cities. The pavilion on the east side of the road would be called *The Pavilion of Jerusalem* and would be, in effect, an enormous indoor fair where merchants and artisans could display their products, traders could meet to transact business, and troupes of entertainers could perform. The pavilion on the west side, *The Pavilion of Jericho*, would contain chambers where those at the higher levels of government, business, religion, and law could be housed and could meet to transact their affairs. Here the great councils and conferences of state would be held, away from the local pressures of either city. And in front of each pavilion would be an enormous statue, one of the Procurator of Jerusalem and the other of the Procurator of Jericho, facing each other across *The Royal Road* like two huge pillars through which travellers would pass with awe.

And finally the most breathtaking idea of all seemed to rise in the minds of several members of the Commission simultaneously. If the road could be resurfaced over its entire length, why couldn't the roadside to a width of several furlongs be landscaped all the way from Jerusalem to Jericho and provide an uninterrupted vista of grass, flowers, fountains, and trees? The phrase which caused the Commission and Procurators to accept this momentous idea was "the longest garden in the world." It would surpass in scope and grandeur the Hanging Gardens of Babylon.

More taxes were levied. Hardly a tree or shrub near either city was safe from being uprooted and transplanted beside the road. Every available stonemason, bricklayer, carpenter, artist, and gardener in both cities was by this time at work on some part of the project. And while taxes were dreadfully heavy, employment was at an all-time high. Also, the two Procurators found other ways to raise revenue. In addition to soliciting loans, gifts, and bribes, they sold work permits and contracts to those engaged in construction; and they sold licenses to the merchants who were vying for future space in the buildings at each campsite and pavilion. As word spread about the project, several foreign powers sent spies. It became necessary to guard all approaches to the road to prevent some foreign power from sabotaging the work or copying the idea, and also to preserve the dramatic impact of the forthcoming Grand Opening.

One of the challenges the Commission faced was the fact that the road, upon emerging from the Gate of Jerusalem, led straight through a sprawling slum, an eyesore which had developed over many years just outside the city's walls. At first the Commission considered razing the entire area, but it was extensive. The cost was prohibitive, and the outcries of hundreds who would thus be dispossessed of their homes could be heard throughout Jerusalem. Then the Commission hit upon a compromise measure. Only those buildings which immediately lined the road would be razed. In order to hide the remainder of the ramshackle area from the view of those on the road, a stone wall the height of two tall men would be built on either side of the road for a length of ten furlongs. By covering much of the wall with flowering vines and planting stately cedars and yews at set intervals, the Commission was able to achieve a magnificent long, narrow avenue which, after ten furlongs, opened into the more spacious garden bordering the road all the rest of the way to Jericho.

It took more than five years to complete the road, and it took every farthing the two Procurators could squeeze from the people. During all this time the Procurators and members of the Royal Commission worked harder than they had ever worked before, riding from one construction site to another, overseeing, directing, and encouraging the huge labor force at work. Often they were away from home for many weeks at a time. Never had they been so happy. And in spite of the fact that their wives, concubines, and mistresses complained of neglect and nearly died of curiosity about the road, the Procurators and the members of the Commission remained faithful to a pact they had made when the project was begun: No one except those directly engaged in work on the road was allowed to see any part of it until the Grand Opening.

And what a Grand Opening it was to be! The plan called for extensive ceremonies in Jerusalem, both religious and secular, followed by a long procession which would travel all the way to Jericho with feasting and revelry at each of the campsites, interrupted by two days of ceremonies, athletic contests, and entertainments at the two pavilions, and finally a Grand Entry into Jericho where welcoming festivities and entertainments would last almost a week.

The procession was to be led by a young man designated "The Universal Traveller," and he was to be the finest example of beauty, manhood, and grace which could be found in the country. Mounted on a white Arabian stallion which had been bred and raised for this purpose, he would break the velvet ribbon across the entrance to the Gate of Jerusalem and ride out upon *The Royal Road*, followed by the royal, the rich, and the famous.

This first contingent of the procession—which was planned to include at least five kings, twelve princes, eight Procurators, and both of the two High Priests, all magnificently mounted—would be followed by a large group of ambassadors from many foreign cities and states, each preceded by the banner he served. The ambassadors would be followed by a great array of priests in their finest robes, all mounted on camels draped in cloth-of-gold. These would be followed by members of the Royal Commission on Commerce riding as a body, or at least as many of them as could still ride, wearing the formal black robes of their office and followed by a brilliant caravan of wagons and sedan chairs carrying the families of all those who preceded.

The caravan of families was to be followed by one hundred foot soldiers with mounted officers, all in new vivid blue uniforms, a gift from the Emperor himself. The soldiers were to be followed by a mounted group of the best athletes in the country, wearing little but their own beautiful bodies, which would be spectacular enough. These were to be followed by a series of flatbed wagons carrying troupes of musicians, dancers, acrobats, and jugglers, performing as the caravan progressed. The entertainers would be followed by nearly everyone in Jerusalem and the outlying areas who could mount a horse, camel, or ass for the occasion; and these by hundreds on foot who had no mounts but wanted to go anyway.

This was the Commission's plan for the Grand Opening; and although there were several attempts to alter it before the great day arrived, it was generally adhered to, since the Commission had by this time become the most powerful arbiter of taste in the country. The two Procurators wanted to scrap this plan and substitute one in which each Procurator led a procession from his own city and the two caravans met at the Pavilions of Jerusalem and Jericho for a grand celebration. But members of the Commission fought this proposed change with all their united strength, and finally won. The idea of a Universal Traveller was very dear to their hearts. And from a more practical standpoint, they feared that a head-on meeting between the citizens from the two cities might lead to a competitive struggle which would ruin the festivities.

Thwarted in this, each of the two Procurators tried to guarantee, by bribery and other means, that his oldest son would be chosen as The Universal Traveller. But the Commission made short work of these attempts, since the son of the Procurator of Jerusalem was notoriously effeminate and the son of the Procurator of Jericho was so ugly, loutish, and ill-smelling that he was commonly called "the Goat Boy of Jericho."

The Commission did, however, make one minor concession. The request came, strangely enough, from the followers of the dead prophet whose story about the Samaritan had figured so prominently in the original Proclamation almost five years earlier. This group had grown into a sizeable if somewhat secretive minority in the meantime. As a religious sect they had no power, but they tended to be considered representatives of the poor; and because of recent taxation policies, the poor now included vast numbers of citizens in both cities. These ragged followers of the dead prophet did not ask to be included in the procession, which the Commission would have prevented at almost any cost, but merely that the Grand Opening include some symbol which they might interpret as a vindication of their dead leader who had been telling the truth about the old road in the first place.

Grasping the irony of the situation and aware of the subtle pressure upon them, the Commission decided to offer these fanatics a symbol which would have no meaning to anyone but them and would be considered only one more flourish by those participating in the procession. It offered to place a Samaritan on either side of the road at intervals of one-half a furlong and for a distance of twenty furlongs beginning at the Gate of Jerusalem. These would represent, to the followers of the prophet, the good Samaritan who had come to the aid of the traveller in the prophet's story. To those in the procession, they would be silent sentries adding to the magnificence of the occasion, like the trees which had been planted along the way. As soon as the procession had passed, they would be paid and dismissed.

In private the Commission agreed that the plan had a certain practical advantage, since it would rid the city for a short but crucial time of some of the half-breed Samaritans who flocked into Jerusalem during any holiday season to beg or steal money, get drunk, and stand about in the streets, impeding traffic and staring at everyone with their strange Babylonian eyes. To the Commission's surprise, the delegation of followers of the dead prophet accepted this proposal without complaint or condition and went away, leaving the members of the Commission to wish all their problems could be so quickly solved, since they had just completed the long and tortuous process of choosing the Universal Traveller.

II

A secret committee had been sent throughout the country to find the most beautiful example of young manhood available. They sought the young man with the clearest eyes, the noblest brow, the broadest shoulders, the narrowest waist, and the most upright carriage. And even though it was a secret committee, its members had to fend off ambitious parents, many of whom were rich and highly placed. But ninety days before the date set for the Grand Opening, the committee narrowed its choices to ten young men and brought them, under the closest security, to a small and obscure village outside Jerusalem where the final judging was to take place and where the young man on whom the choice fell would be housed in secrecy until the day of the Grand Opening.

The entire Commission on Commerce acted as the final judges. The ten young candidates, carefully groomed for the competition, were identified to members of the Commission only by number so that none of the judges would be influenced by which city or family any of them represented. They were led into the judging area nearly naked and paraded before the Commission for several hours while the judges prodded and pinched them to determine muscle tone, measured their shoulders and waists, examined their teeth, and stared at them from every possible angle. Each young man took his turn riding a horse past the judges, and each demonstrated his strength, grace of movement, and stamina by lifting to his shoulder a heavy urn filled with

65

water and holding it there during a count of 1,000 without spilling a drop.

When the secret ballots were counted, the eighteen-year-old son of a wine merchant from Joppa had won by a comfortable margin. The young man was led back into the judging area, congratulated by the entire Commission, anointed by a priest, given his sacred charge, and led away as The Universal Traveller, the most envied young man in the country. Then the members of the Commission returned to Jerusalem, happy with their choice and well aware that much money would be changing hands as that choice became known. Wagers, throughout the country and as far away as Rome, had been running three-to-one that the winner would be a blond with green eyes, the Hellenistic ideal. But the young man from Joppa had shoulder-length tawny chestnut hair and eyes as blue as the Lake of Genesaret. And as they were riding back to Jerusalem, the members of the Commission were also more aware than they had ever been of their wrinkles, paunches, and gray hair.

What they were not aware of was that the young man they had just chosen for this great honor had developed his impressive shoulders by lifting huge vats of wine in his father's shop, and that he had developed his irresistable expression of dazed and dazzling innocence by a considerable involvement with the product of that same shop. But the two trustworthy eunuchs, in whose care he was placed until the day of the Grand Opening, found out soon enough. It was their job to keep him healthy and, above all else, beautiful until that great day. It proved to be a more difficult task than they had anticipated.

He was homesick and did not like confinement. It seemed that everywhere he turned a fat eunuch was offering him food or trying to comb his hair. He missed his father and still more his father's shop. Even the many young girls whom the giggling eunuchs provided for him did not slake his thirst for wine. He threw temper tantrums and threatened to starve himself or scar his face if he were not given more wine. He refused to bathe or care for himself in any way; and once, when one of his keepers was attempting to brush his teeth, he bit the eunuch's finger off and spat it in his face. At such times, four strong men were called in to subdue him. Only by heroic efforts, including the use of force and whatever diversionary tactics they could employ, were the eunuchs able to keep his intake of wine at a reasonable level and his beautiful face and body in their original condition.

But early on the morning of the Grand Opening, when the celebration had been going on in Jerusalem for several days and the city was crowded with thousands who had come to catch a glimpse of this paragon as he spurred his white stallion forward onto *The Royal Road*, the eunuchs realized that they had met their match and that this paragon's capacity for wine was equalled only by his cunning. He simply refused to go. He would have to be carried, thrust on his horse, and held there, unless he were given wine. As the hour of his scheduled departure drew nearer, the frantic eunuchs looked deep into one another's eyes and made their decision.

The Universal Traveller arrived at his appointed position just inside the Gate of Jerusalem exactly on time. He sat his horse like an emperor, and the sunlight reflecting from his burnished chestnut hair was almost blinding. Many in the crowd gasped at his beauty; and where his gaze of incredible innocence and strength fell upon them, they strained forward as if to receive a blessing. He was wearing the long, diamond-studded purple cloak of Herod the Great, and the ancient sword at his side was the most treasured secular relic the country possessed.

He was radiant, beautiful, magnificent—everything the Commission had hoped for. And he was gloriously drunk.

The procession, already formed and waiting for the sound of horns which would signal it to begin, extended back from the Gate of Jerusalem and down one of the city's narrow streets for more than eight furlongs. In the Caravan of Families, great ladies were counting their children and cushions, giving last-minute instructions to servants about adjusting sunshades, and trying to think of what they might have forgotten but would need, terribly, during the next few days. On the flatbed wagons of the entertainers, dancers were stretching and practicing leaps while rows of harpists were tuning their tall harps as if caressing them, oblivious to the noise and confusion around them.

The top of the city wall as well as every side street, rooftop, balcony, and window nearby was crowded with spectators straining to see The Universal Traveller. The weather was perfect: a bright sunny day with just enough breeze to keep the flags and banners flying. The final speech by the Procurator of Jerusalem, who had been carefully advised on this by members of the Commission, was blessedly brief. From a platform built for the purpose, one of the High Priests placed a gold chain over the head of the mounted Universal Traveller and affixed to it the official symbol of peace and prosperity, a sunburst of gold and nacre in whose center gleamed the largest sapphire known to exist outside of Rome. The other High Priest placed on his finger an ancient ring set with a fiery opal the size of a large olive and said to have been worn by King Melchizedek, who had neither beginning nor end.

The two Procurators and the two High Priests kissed the ring, bowed to the Universal Traveller, and took their places in the first section of the procession, which was to follow him at a distance of one furlong. Then, with a quick flourish of his jewelled hand in the direction of the trumpeters above him on the gate, and an accompanying fanfare, The Universal Traveller urged his horse forward, broke the velvet ribbon, and passed through the Gate of Jerusalem while the crowd cheered until the buildings vibrated and echoed as if with the roar of an avalanche.

He emerged from the gate onto the long avenue with its high stone wall on either side designed to shut out the view of the slums outside Jerusalem. As far as he could see ahead the walls were covered with vines bearing large yellow blossoms, and at intervals of one-half furlong a Samaritan stood at attention on either side of the road, each holding a traveller's staff which had been provided for the occasion. As he passed the second pair of Samaritans, the first contingent of the procession, including Royalty, Procurators, and the two High Priests, emerged from the gate behind him; and behind them came the next group, the ambassadors preceded by flag bearers. Each group had been instructed to stay one furlong behind the preceding group.

What happened next has been differently reported by different witnesses, but there is no dispute about where it happened, since the Universal Traveller had just passed the sixteenth pair of Samaritans and was still in view of the cheering multitude on top of the city wall. Some of these said they saw a small piece of white parchment or fragment of a papyrus scroll blown by the wind in front of the Universal Traveller's horse. Others said it was a bit of lace or a white handkerchief belonging to one of the brilliantly dressed ladies in the Caravan of Families, just at this moment emerging from the gate. Later, there were other and less simple explanations, but whatever the cause, the magnificent white stallion was frightened by something. Suddenly he shied, reared, and began to paw the air. And before anyone could realize what was happening, the Universal Traveller fell from the horse and lit on his head in the middle of the road, evidently breaking his beautiful neck.

For a few seconds, during which the horrified spectators on the wall stood as if turned to stone and the first section of the procession faltered in confusion, blood spurted from a gash in the young man's throat, splashing onto the head and chest of the stallion, which continued to rear and plunge above him. Then the bloodstained stallion turned and galloped, wild-eyed and terrified, back the way he had come.

Seeing the bloody stallion bearing down upon them as if chased by a devil, those in the first group of the procession a furlong behind the Universal Traveller—the Royal, the rich, and the famous—lost their composure entirely. One of them (perhaps one of the kings or princes who were not known for bravery under the best of circumstances) began to scream, "The road is cursed! The road is cursed!" Others shouted, "Demons! There are demons on the road!" In a panic they turned their horses and began to retreat at full speed toward the gate. The superstitious Samaritans also fled toward the gate, using their staffs to knock anything or anybody out of their way. The ambassadors, who made up the second contingent of the procession, although many of them did not understand the language well enough to know what was being shouted, recognized the fear of those racing toward them. When their flag bearers dropped the flags in panic, they too turned their horses and joined the mad flight toward the gate.

But only a furlong in front of them was the group of over fifty priests, including the entire Sanhedrin, now frantically trying to turn their cumbersome camels around and make their own retreat. The first two groups collided with the priests in a wild melee of screaming men, bellowing animals, and tangled harnesses.

Hampered by their trailing robes, which caught in the stirrups of the horses sweeping past them, several of the priests were pulled from their camels and trampled. Three camels fell, throwing their riders into the path of the oncoming horses; and several of the horses, attempting to leap over the fallen camels, fell also.

This collision provided the next group, the Royal Commission on Commerce, with a few more seconds to get their horses turned around and headed at full speed back toward the gate. But their situation proved to be even worse than that of the priests; for the driver of the huge and ornate wagon carrying the family of the Procurator of Jerusalem, when he heard the cries and saw the surge of men and animals coming toward him, had attempted to turn his wagon around in the narrow space and had turned it over. It lay on its side, forming a barricade behind which those members of the Procurator's family who were not too badly injured or frightened were attempting to extricate themselves from a tangle of tapestries, servants, and cushions. Just as the members of the Commission, in full flight, reached this barricade, the confused mass of men on horses and camels who had survived the earlier collision caught up with them. While some were able to guide their mounts through the narrow spaces left at either end of the wagon, many could not control their frightened animals and slammed into the wagon at a gallop, turning it over onto its top with its wheels in the air and trapping the occupants beneath it. The next onslaught—the Royal, the rich, and the famous—rode directly over the wagon, leaving it nearly flat.

Only about half the wagons and sedan chairs in the Caravan of Families had emerged from the gate when the panic first broke out. The fate of those trapped in the narrow passageway of the gate itself was ghastly. Most of them were trampled beyond recognition, and nothing

71

was left of their wagons and sedan chairs except a layer of debris scattered over the road, partially covering their mutilated bodies. A few of the wagons which had not yet entered the gate were able to avoid destruction by turning into the side streets which crossed the main route of the procession, but they were able to do this only by plunging through the press of spectators who filled the streets; and once they had done so, they blocked the side exits for others attempting to follow

The first to fight their way back through the gate were about thirty wild-eyed Samaritans. Clearing the way before them with their staffs, they burst upon the band of foot soldiers following the Caravan of Families and just inside the gate. The officers, who could not see beyond the gate but could hear confused screams and shouts, assumed that the Samaritans had taken this opportunity to sack the city, a fear that was always present. Immediately they gave the command for their soldiers to draw swords and fight. The Samaritans, outnumbered and with only their staffs, would have been no match for the soldiers except that they were very agile and each of them seemed to be carrying, somewhere under his cloak, a long knife which he used with alarming accuracy.

But the battle was brief because it was only a few moments before the first wave of the retreating procession—a wild phalanx of horses, camels, and wagons—bore down upon it. In the confusion before they fled or were trampled, the soldiers found themselves fighting priests, members of the Commission, ambassadors, and various among the Royal, the rich, and the famous. One soldier realized, to his horror and only a fraction of a second too late, that he had just run his sword through the ample abdomen of a Hasmonean King. He quickly withdrew his sword, propped the body against the nearest wall, and fled in the direction of the general stampede, hoping no one would notice the King's fixed expression and glassy eyes.

The street inside the gate was much narrower than the road on the outside. It was filled with the rest of the procession waiting to move through the gate in their turn: a band of mounted athletes followed by a dozen large wagons carrying musicians and entertainers and, behind these, several hundred citizens on horses, camels, oxen, and asses followed by hundreds more on foot. When the athletes heard the cries and saw the battle between soldiers and Samaritans directly in front of them, they stopped in amazement. The musicians on the wagons behind them, still unaware of what was happening, continued to play. But as soon as the athletes saw the possessed riders sweeping over everything in their path as the tide sweeps over a sandbar, they turned and whipped their horses back the way they had come. Impeded by the wagons of the entertainers, they were soon overtaken by the mad crush of horses and camels. Then the surviving wagons from the Caravan of Families thundered down upon them with passengers peering from behind ripped tapestries and shrieking, "Demons! Demons! They are behind us."

A wagon carrying the most famous troupe of dancers in the country was overturned, and girls in harem trousers and veils fled from the wreckage only to be run down by mounted men, some of them priests who had managed to retain their dizzying perches high on their camels by discarding their outer garments along the way. Some of the dancers, as quick of mind as they were nimble-footed, leaped onto passing riderless horses and were carried to safety. Others were less fortunate.

The mounted citizens were overtaken before they could get their animals turned around and headed in the opposite direction. Those who were caught in mid-turn were struck broadside and knocked into a heap where they were trampled before they could regain their footing. Those who managed to avoid being knocked down turned their mounts and joined the mass of riders and wagons plunging toward the citizens on foot. Here the slaughter was greatest; for although some of the luckier ones were able to duck into doorways, leap through windows, or even climb the walls, most were unable to save themselves from the galloping flood which bore down upon them, trapped as they were in the narrow street. Throngs of spectators on the roofs and balconies watched the carnage with horror, screaming warnings to those below, but their screams were unheard above the general din of panic, suffering, and death.

No accurate count of how many died that day was ever made, but even a conservative estimate would place the number at more than 1,000, and the number of injured and maimed is beyond estimation. There was hardly a family in Jerusalem without losses. The surrounding towns and villages had so many mourning families that for years afterward when anyone died in these outlying regions, that person was said to have "gone to Jerusalem."

Those who were killed within the city walls, often mangled beyond identification, were gathered up for burial in mass graves. But all afternoon of that black day the people feared the road so much they would not venture out through the gate to rescue the injured and retrieve the bodies of the dead scattered on *The Royal Road* amid carcasses of horses and camels and the bloody wreckage of wagons and sedan chairs. Soldiers maintained a vigil from the top of the city gate; and from time to time a discarded robe or a tattered banner would rise in the breeze and hover over the road like a huge bird of prey until it settled on a dead horse or caught in the vines along one of the walls. The ghostly cries of those who lay on the road, still alive but too badly injured to crawl back into the city, rose as the cries of souls in torment.

Finally, while there was still time before sunset, a

centurion and thirty of his armed men went out on the road to rescue the injured and retrieve the bodies of the dead. It was the same centurion and some of the same soldiers who, more than six years earlier, had scourged the old road of bandits. The dangers of that mission had been nothing to them compared to the dangers of this one; but they performed it, looking often over their shoulders and fearing the sun would set before they were done. To be out on that road in daylight was terrifying; to be there after dark was unthinkable. They threw the dead and the living together into wagons and bolted back through the gate with such haste that some of the injured did not survive their rescue. And early the next morning a crew of stone-masons appeared at the Gate of Jerusalem. They worked steadily all day, and by night-fall they had sealed the gate with large stones.

The losses among the notables were recorded. They included more than half of the Commission on Commerce, twenty-two priests, fifteen ambassadors, three procurators, six princes, one high priest, and one king. Oddly enough, the body of the King, of the Hasmonean Royal Family, was not found until the next day when a woman complained to a passing soldier that there was a naked madman standing in front of her house. When the soldier investigated, he found the King, rigid in death, stripped of his jewels and rich clothing, propped against the wall with a Samaritan's staff, and staring at the world in haughty amazement.

The scores of dead from the Caravan of Families included the Procurator of Jerusalem's wife, two daughters, youngest son, and three grandchildren. Later, in official speeches, he often compared his fate to that of Job, and with much justification. But the Procurator and his eldest son escaped destruction.

When the bloodstained white stallion bore down upon them, the Procurator did not panic, as others in the first group of the procession did. Calling to his son to follow, he drew his horse close in against the wall and let the stallion pass. Then, at his direction, the two of them spurred their horses forward toward the Universal Traveller. By the time they reached his body, the stampede toward the gate was well underway, and no one noticed them as they dismounted and examined the fallen youth. Even in death he was beautiful, although he smelled strongly of wine; but there were other things about him that interested the Procurator more.

The Procurator knew every detail of this stretch of the road, and he knew that the walls on either side extended only two furlongs farther and then gave way to a garden from which they could easily go back into the city through another gate. And only an idiot would attempt to fight his way back into the city through the slaughter and confusion between them and the Gate of Jerusalem. And so, with the body of the Universal Traveller slung across the Procurator's horse, they made their way to the end of the walls and back into the city on back streets through the slums. Once within the city walls, amid the bodies of the dead and the screams of the dying, no one paid any attention to them, muddy and bloodstained as they were. They decided, in the light of what had happened, to bury the Universal Traveller's body as quickly and quietly as possible. This they did in a secluded spot on the outskirts of the city, digging the grave themselves with spades they had borrowed from the owner of an olive grove.

In the weeks to come there were official inquiries, which the Procurator of Jerusalem himself directed, but no one was able to ascertain what had become of the fortune in jewels and the priceless sword the Universal Traveller was wearing when he fell, so precipitously, from his horse. Nor was his body ever found, although that was a matter of less concern except to his family and later historians. The diamonds were never heard of again, but years afterward the sword and the opal ring turned up in the hands of unscrupulous traders in Syria and Mesopotamia; and rumor said that the sapphire, in a different setting, had been seen on the throat of a Persian Princess. But none of these treasures were returned because no later administration could afford to buy them back.

III

Even before the stampede through the city had run its course, the band of Samaritans appropriated riderless horses and fled into the desert toward their homeland. They had seen enough of high culture for one day. Using old trails they knew well from an earlier time when they had made their living in the vicinity of the Jericho Road disguised as the dreaded Sicarii, they approached Jericho at dusk and decided to spend the night there, since it would give them the opportunity to get drunk. The citizens of Jericho were celebrating and preparing for the procession's Triumphal Entry into the city, which was to take place in three days. When the Samaritans told their story, confusion spread throughout Jericho. And although many of the citizens and officials did not want to believe these shifty-eyed half-breeds, they could not deny that the terror with which the Samaritans described the ghosts and demons on the road was unfeigned.

Next morning the top of the city wall near the Gate of Jericho was crowded with people staring down *The Royal Road*, fearful of what they might see. Each time a dust devil appeared in the distance, they scrambled down from the wall and took refuge behind bolted doors in the buildings nearby, only to creep back later and take up their positions on the wall. At midmorning an official messenger from Jerusalem limped in, exhausted. He had become lost twice in the night while crossing the desert, and his attempts to stay as far away from *The Royal Road* as possible had led him through such unfamiliar and barren country that his horse was almost dead of thirst. He verified everything the Samaritans had said, and added dimensions to the slaughter which they had neglected to mention.

The people of Jericho were dazed and confused. The Procurator called a hasty meeting of city officials. Afterward, a crew of stonemasons worked all night by torchlight and under close guard. By dawn the magnificent Gate of Jericho was sealed and the entire city had gone into mourning for the fallen citizens of Jerusalem.

And the *Royal Road* was never reopened. In both cities it came to be known as "the Road of Blood." Later it was generally referred to as "Fools Road," since only a fool would venture upon it. Terrible stories of those who attempted to use the road or even stumbled upon it by accident were common everywhere. The people's belief that the road was haunted was unshakable, although they were not all in agreement as to what it was haunted by. The most persistent story was that anyone who attempted to use the road simply vanished; and there was probably some truth in this since, as the country came to be administered by increasingly weak Prefects and Procurators, banditry and even the Sicarii again flourished.

Gradually it came to be rumored that the white object which had fluttered in front of the Universal Traveller's horse, causing it to rear, had been the ghost of the dead prophet who had told the original story about the Jericho Road and who, as his followers remembered, had always worn robes of purest white. Another persistent belief originated with one of the eyewitnesses on the Wall of Jerusalem. He said that during the stampede toward the gate, he had seen the body of the Universal Traveller rising directly into heaven in a blaze of light. And since the body had vanished mysteriously, many believed that the beautiful young man had been translated into heaven in this miraculous manner.

The only people who did not believe the road was haunted were the Idumean horse traders from Arabia, who brought their mares and stallions to northern markets each year. They laughed at the entire story. It was obvious to them what had made the Universal Traveller's horse shy and rear. Any finely-bred Arabian horse, they said, grows nervous in the presence of Samaritans, since these horses have keen instincts concerning human character, and they know that the only good Samaritan is a dead Samaritan.

But the gates remained sealed, and the ghosts of those who had died on the road were said to wander endlessly from one gate to the other. Sometimes they could be heard at night crying piteously for entrance to Jerusalem or Jericho.

And it was a bad time for the country in general, drained as it was of resources, its main trade route paralyzed, and with many of its leaders, both secular and religious, wiped out in one day. Soon the Procurator of Jerusalem retired to his luxurious villa outside Rome, and the Prefect sent to replace him was little more than a clerk. He had no real interest in or knowledge of the people; and he immediately ran afoul of the Priesthood, which in those troubled times had grown more powerful and so conservative as to be considered, by Roman officials, fanatical. The experiment in Hellenization had failed, and it had failed in such a dramatic way that the people turned to their old beliefs with increased tenacity. Unfortunately, those beliefs were not designed to make the country a docile and productive province of Rome.

The Empire itself was lurching through the first century toward its own collapse. Beleaguered from

79

without and rotting from within, it flailed wildly from side to side, like a drunken giant attacked by a swarm of mosquitoes. Its leaders, ever less farsighted and effective than their predecessors, had little time or patience for a stiff-necked people in a tiny province who had tied up most of the country's wealth in a single road and then were too superstitious to use it. And the Province, even in palmier days, had never been a particularly profitable investment for the Empire. Then, in the year 68, the disastrous Jewish Wars began, and two years later a Roman Legion marched into Jerusalem, razed the Temple, killed most of the priests, and destroyed the city, leaving the people prostrate and powerless. This, the second major disaster within twenty years, effectively truncated the historical continuity of an entire people.

But there was one minority, the followers of the dead prophet, who survived with their spirits and determination intact. The sect had grown and was spreading out from Jerusalem. Its members came to be called "Christians," a term of derision, and were often legislated against and persecuted. But the very illegality of the sect was a factor in its survival since the men, although sometimes imprisoned for their religious beliefs, were never conscripted for military service and did not involve themselves in the country's futile struggles with Rome. As persecution increased and war raged, the Christians withdrew more and more from society and lived in small bands, often hidden in the hills outside Jerusalem. These bands, which were generally left undisturbed during the war and afterwards, grew and became cells of learning and intellectual ferment. As well as the teachings of their dead prophet, the Christians made use of the work of several Greek philosophers of an earlier period, especially the work of Plato. And gradually a curious phenomenon occurred which was just one more chapter in the old story about necessity being the mother of invention.

Because these bands of Christians were widely scattered in a war-torn land and their members could not go about the country without fear of being imprisoned or even killed, they communicated with one another by means of letters. They developed a veritable underground railroad through which letters from the leader of one group could be smuggled to the members of another. The letters, which taught, encouraged, and directed members of the sect, insured a uniformity of dogma and spirit and served in lieu of the direct discourse of religious leaders. The writers of these letters, self-educated men for the most part, through study and practice came to be masters of the Greek vernacular then in use.

And in time several of them wrote histories of the sect, which purported to be factual and were to have a great effect upon the future of philosophical and religious thought. But the events they were attempting to describe had happened many years earlier, and they were neither eye-witnesses nor trained historians and had no access to written records. They did have access to the verbal accounts and stories with which real events become so quickly overlaid, and they wrote from a certain bias and from a belief in religious mysticism. Their histories are brilliant examples of what time does to the past, how it merges and transforms events, sometimes placing the wrong characters in the right setting, or telescopes incidents which happened years apart.

It was only a short step from the belief that the dead prophet's ghost had been seen on *The Royal Road* and the body of the Universal Traveller had been carried directly into heaven, to the compressed version that the prophet's body had been seen ascending into heaven at the same place just outside Jerusalem. And the two figures, both of whom had captured the popular imagination, merged in other ways. In attempting to describe or paint portraits of the dead prophet, whom they had never seen, his later followers drew upon the stereotyped description of the Universal Traveller. And thus, Jesus of Nazareth, of whose actual appearance we know absolutely nothing, has come to be thought of as tall and slender with shoulder-length chestnut hair and incredibly blue eyes. Centuries after the Universal Traveller and his brief, sad history have been forgotten, his features are seen constantly in the religious portraiture of the Western World. Such are the ways of history. But both he and the road died young, while they were still beautiful.

The gates remained sealed. Gradually the flumes collapsed and the streams dried up. The trees and plants along the road died from lack of water, and the desert returned to claim this narrow strip which had once been "the longest garden in the world." The pavilions and the buildings at each campsite became the homes of snakes, lizards, and wild dogs who roamed the area without fear of man. Sand dunes moved across the road so that if anyone had been there to see it, it would have looked like a stone ribbon which often disappeared into a mountain of sand as if into a tunnel, only to reappear on the other side.

The massive statues of the Procurators in front of the pavilions remained for many years, eroded by blowing sand until one could not have been told from the other. Eventually they collapsed from the pressure of a sand dune moving slowly over them. The pieces into which they broke were rolled along inside the dune as if in a slowly moving sea, until the dune moved on and left them behind as perfectly smooth pieces of stone scattered over the floor of the desert. The head of one of the statues was found by a band of barbarians who were sweeping over the land from far to the north and east. These primitive tribesmen were puzzled by the smooth, round stone, which they thought must have been shaped and placed there by some earlier inhabitants of this deserted place. Hoping it might contain something of value, they broke it open and found it to be quite hollow.

BIOGRAPHICAL NOTE

Richard Shelton was born and grew up in Boise, Idaho. He has lived in southern Arizona since 1956, where he teaches in the Creative Writing Program at the University of Arizona in Tucson. He is the author of 13 collections of poetry, including *Selected Poems: 1969-1981* (University of Pittsburgh Press). This is his first book of prose.